The Wallace House of Pain

A Novelette

S.M. STEVENS

ISBN: 979-8-8689-0863-7

Cover design by: Natalie Simone
@nootcreations

Library of Congress Control Number: 2018675309

Printed in the United States of America

CONTENTS

DINNER #1

In the passenger seat of Terrance's black Prius, Xander jiggled his leg, but not in time to the music. Guilt niggled his conscience. "Remember what I relayed when I extended this invitation—we don't choose our parents. My Dad isn't the most liberal guy in the world."

Terrance kept his eyes peeled for Mill Street. "I'm sure I've handled worse in thirty years. But if he's so bad, why are you dragging me with you?"

Xander watched his fingers drumming on his thigh. "Truth be told, having someone else there prevents the conversation from devolving into a farce of familial relations." He breathed on the side window as the streets of the modest city borough slipped by. "In other words, it sucks and I need moral support." He drew a peace sign on the window. "It's that beige one on the right."

Terrance parked at the curb in front of a well-tended triple-decker. Early evening sun bounced off small rectangles of trim lawn on either side of the front walkway. He grabbed a six-pack from the back seat and followed

Xander up three steps to the front door, which opened as they neared.

"Hello, hello," sang Kathy, the statuesque, buffed and blow-dried hairdresser who became Xander's stepmother less than a year after his mother died from pneumonia. "How are you?"

Xander looked down at Kathy's manicured, pearly-pink fingernails digging into his arm. "Reasonable."

She lowered her voice. "I'm so glad you came. These monthly dinners mean a lot to Jim." Her voice returned to normal. "I know you had to work late, so I've got supper all ready. Hungry?" Without waiting for a reply, she pulled him inside and repeated the maneuver with Terrance.

"And you're Terrance, of course. I love your hair."

Terrance's hand reflexively touched his close-cropped, blonde-dyed hair.

"I love the contrast with your skin color."

Xander rolled his eyes behind Kathy's back.

Terrance winced infinitesimally and adjusted his heavy, black-framed glasses. "Well, I'm glad you like it. Unlike my skin color, I did pick out the hair color," he deadpanned.

"You're funny!" Kathy hooted. "I'm a hair stylist, you know." She patted her honey-colored updo with one hand, took the six-pack of beer with the other and led them to the dining room. "Maybe I can do your hair sometime."

"No offense, Mrs. Wallace, but my mother always told me never let a white person touch my hair."

Xander started to laugh but swallowed it—his father had entered the room. Jim Wallace stood an inch shorter than Xander but weighed fifty pounds more. His ruddy face, beefy hands and constantly shifting blue eyes gave the appearance of a boxer in a ring. Xander gauged the amount of gray in his father's brown hair and wondered when his own hair would start showing its age.

"Dad."

"Alex."

Jim strode toward Terrance, his impressive bulk seeming to part the air in the room, whipping up an invisible maelstrom.

"Terrance Washington, sir. Pleased to meet you." Terrance extended a hand.

Xander watched Jim's flinty eyes take in all of Terrance in one thorough assessment, from his six feet of height and blonde dye job, hefty glasses and diamond stud earrings to his burnt umber-colored skin and his black shirt, pants and shoes. Jim released a barely audible grunt as he shook hands.

"Come on, let's eat." He glanced at his wristwatch. "Kathy, can you get the food going sometime this century?"

Xander squinted, unclear—as was often the case—if his father was irritated or unsuccessfully attempting lighthearted sarcasm.

"It's all ready, Jim, I'll get it now."

Kathy's submissive tone irritated Xander—his mother never let Jim roll over her like that.

While Kathy ferried steaming dishes of meatloaf, gravy, mashed potatoes, carrots and green beans between the kitchen and dining room, Terrance looked at his friend across the table and raised an eyebrow. "Alex?"

Xander looked up in an appeal to the heavens.

Jim looked Terrance square in the eye. "That's his name. It's a perfectly good one, picked out by his mother, and I see no reason to change it."

"You see, Terrance," Xander said, refusing to look at his father, "even at twenty-eight, I'm apparently not mature enough to select the moniker I prefer. So here I remain Alex whilst everywhere else, I am Xander."

Kathy came in gripping three beer bottles by their necks, like a jangling upside-down bouquet. "Look, Jim, Terrance brought us some beer. Who's having one?"

Xander took two and passed one to Terrance.

Jim frowned at the label. "I'll have my usual."

Kathy scurried back to the kitchen and returned seconds later with a Bud Lite.

"My father thinks drinking imported beer converts previously respectable God-fearing citizens into socialists and iconoclasts. Never mind that Anheuser-Busch is owned by a Belgian-Brazilian company now."

Jim made a *pfft* noise. "But it's still brewed here."

Terrance quickly swigged from his beer. "No worries, it's all good."

After a silence interrupted only by serving spoons clinking against bowls and plates, Kathy cleared her throat. "Terrance, so you work with Alex at the Wildlife Preservation—what is it again?"

"The Wilderness Protection Society." Terrance dug into the mashed potatoes. "I moved here to take the job six months ago."

Jim finished ladling carrots onto his plate and thudded the bowl down in the middle of the table. "So, you're a tree-hugger too."

The corner of Terrance's mouth twitched. "Well, sir, I do believe the human race is destroying the planet and if we don't change our ways soon, the Earth won't sustain future generations."

Xander smiled into his plate.

"I think this global warming stuff is a bunch of BS. How

can it be getting warmer if it's snowing more than ever and some winters are colder than a witch's tit?" He focused his beady eyes on Terrance.

"It's simple science, actually. Warmer temperatures mean more moisture in the air which means—"

"Terrance," Xander cut in, stabbing the air with his fork. "Conserve your breath."

"Anyway, I thought your job," Jim said, looking directly at Xander, "was to save the birds and the bees or some such shit."

"Jim, language," Kathy admonished. "Alex has explained this before. To save the animals, you have to save the planet too." She tossed an ingratiating smile Xander's way. "Terrance, why don't you tell us what you do at work?"

Terrance swallowed his mouthful and put down his fork. "Sure. Like everyone at Wilderness Protection, my job revolves around monitoring what's going on with the climate and the environment, and motivating people to make positive changes to lessen our impact on the natural world."

Jim speared a bite of meatloaf.

"My focus is communications. Xander's actually got the more important job, because he's on the front lines organizing the masses and holding the bad guys accountable for their misdeeds."

Xander knew where Terrance's attempt at support would lead, and his father did not disappoint.

"And by 'misdeeds' you mean somebody trying to make an honest living," Jim stated.

Xander sighed and scratched his short beard. "No, Dad, he means people like the developer Liam Flammer, who gleefully circumvents environmental regulations whenever he pleases to convert another piece of pristine wilderness into condos or a factory. We're fighting Flammer right now on—"

Jim slammed his fork down on the table. "And what's wrong with factories? They give a lot of hard-working people decent jobs."

"My dad's a supervisor at the paper mill."

Terrance nodded. "Nothing's wrong with factories per se—we need them. But there are plenty of brownfield sites that could be used to site new factories and other big projects instead of ruining undeveloped wilderness."

"Brownfield? What the hell is a brownfield? Sounds shitty to me." Jim laughed, sending a burst of sour air into his son's face. Xander shut his eyes against the assault.

They ate, mostly in silence, until Kathy stood and gathered a few dishes. "I'm going to warm up the dessert."

Terrance rose, plate in hand. "Let me help."

Kathy opened her mouth to refuse the offer, but Jim silenced her with one look.

"Go on and help, son." He waited for Terrance and Kathy to disappear. "Alex, how long are you going to keep this up?"

Xander's shoulders dropped a hitch. "What, Dad? What is it this time?" He tried to stare his father down but, as usual, broke his gaze first.

"The job. When are you going to get a real job at a real company? Stop thinking about yourself and plan for your future. That means you might have to have a job you *care* less about," he said with sarcastic emphasis, "but that puts you in a better position to provide for a family."

Xander's face flushed. "I've told you myriad times. For a nonprofit, Wilderness Protection compensates well and offers substantial benefits. It *is* a legitimate job and the person I marry will understand that and support my career choice."

"No, you don't get it," Jim said, starting a familiar refrain. "It's not all about you. The world doesn't revolve around you. Sometimes you have to do things you don't want to do."

Xander picked up the saltshaker and shook it numerous times over the flowered tablecloth. He pushed the crystals together with his finger and started dividing them into tiny hills.

"All you millennials are the same. Everyone's special," Jim said in a mocking tone. "Everyone gets a trophy just for showing up. Everyone's entitled to whatever they want. Well, guess what? Life isn't like that, and the sooner you realize it, the better off you'll be."

Xander clamped his teeth and stiffened his shoulders against the tirade. Jim's criticisms of millennials always felt like an attack on the parenting choices made by Xander's mother. Xander refused to sully her memory by dragging her into the conversation.

"Your generation had it so easy because your mother did everything for you. When I was a kid, I mowed lawns and delivered newspapers to make a buck and get the things I wanted. We didn't sit around on our asses all day on Facebook and whatever else it is you use. By the time I was your age, I had a wife and three kids to feed. That makes you grow up real fast. You could—"

The kitchen door swung open, cutting short Jim's tirade against Xander's life choices as Kathy and Terrance returned. Thankfully, Xander thought, his dad showed enough decorum to clam up, keeping the subject of his son's dreadful prospects in the family.

Jim shifted to face their guest, draping his arm across the back of his chair as if preparing to ask about Sunday's football game. Xander squirmed in his seat.

"What's up with the hair, son? And the earrings?"

"His name is Terrance, Dad."

"He knows who I'm talking to. Don't you?"

Terrance nodded, eyes narrowing.

"You trying to make a statement? Is that what all the, you know, certain types of guys wear these days?"

Xander's eyes widened as he caught his father's inference. "Are you asking if he's gay? Don't you think that's a rather personal question to ask a guest?"

"I'm just curious. I don't have anything against the fa— against the homosexuals, isn't that right, Kathy?"

His wife nodded. "We think one of the guys on Jim's crew is gay," she offered. "And he's got Mexicans, African-Americans and, what is it, Jim?—oh right, Brazilians working for him, too," she added, as if Jim's multinational, ethnically mixed crew somehow added weight to his claim of sexual orientation tolerance.

"That's right. And no one makes a big deal of it. As long as he gets his job done, and as long as he's not illegal, I don't care what color he is or who he—who he spends time with."

"And with that ringing endorsement, the world's gay and minority populations sighed in relief." Xander gestured with his arms for emphasis like a speaker on a stage.

"Alex, why are you so angry?" Kathy turned in her seat to face him. "You're the one who brought it up."

Xander stood and put his paper napkin on his plate. "I'm not angry. I'm exceptionally disinterested because the conversation here never changes. But thank you for dinner,

Kathy. It was delectable. A pleasure as always." He made a slight bow in his stepmother's direction.

"But we have brownies and ice cream," Kathy protested. "The brownies should be warm now."

Xander pleaded to Terrance with his eyes. Terrance sniffed the chocolatey air, smiled wistfully, and stood up. "Smells great but I'm watching my figure."

Jim grimaced.

"Okay, until next time then," Xander tossed over his shoulder as he fled the house, taking the three front steps in one jump and only inhaling again once he settled into the passenger seat of Terrance's car.

He exhaled, running a hand through his shaggy, dirty-blonde hair, his features loosening. "At least he didn't admonish me to get a haircut."

Terrance pulled away from the curb. "'Not the most liberal guy'? You could have been more specific, like—for starters—warning me he was a climate change denier."

Xander pulled his lips back in fake consternation. "But then I would have had to warn you he's also a racist, a sexist, a xenophobe and a homophobe, and the ride here wasn't nearly long enough for all that."

"I'm glad you think this is funny. You basically threw me to the wolves, pitched me in the lion's den, dangled me out there like bait."

The earlier modicum of guilt wormed its way back into Xander's consciousness and bloomed into a healthy helping of remorse, so much so that he abstained from commenting on Terrance's appalling use of clichés. For the first time that night, he looked at Terrance as his friend, not a shield.

"I am truly sorry for putting you in that position. I let my trepidation skew my moral code, and I apologize."

Terrance sighed. "It's all right."

Xander chuckled and started counting on his fingers. "I don't know which alarmed him more—the hair, the earrings, the tree-hugging job or your race."

Terrance lobbed an annoyed glance over to his friend. "You suck, you know that?"

"So tell me, why did you adopt the bottle-blonde effect anyway?"

Terrance looked at the side mirror, the radio, and the road slipping away in front of him.

"That's a story for another day. For now, let's just say it helps me stand out."

"Hmm. I have to say, if you're striving to stand out, you might wear something besides black once in a while." Xander stroked his multi-colored, tie-dyed T-shirt for emphasis.

"Naw, women love this mysterious look. But can I ask you something now?" Xander gave a nod of permission. "Why do you keep going to these dinners?"

Xander pursed his lips. "I guess because I'm the only one he's got. One of my sisters moved three states away and the other one stopped coming several months back. She says it's too arduous to pack up her husband and two kids for a quick meal."

As Terrance parked in front of a somewhat dilapidated two-story house converted to apartments, Xander closed his eyes and drawled as if in a trance. "*Intolerance reigns, in the Wallace house of pain. Will peace ever come?*"

Terrance stared at Xander. "What do you call those little ditties again?"

"A haiku, dude. It's not a ditty. A ditty is a song."

"Remind me why you find satisfaction in making up one

of the world's shortest poems?"

Xander wriggled and stretched his shoulders. "I don't seek them out. They pop into my head when I least expect it. I've had this affliction since fifth grade when I penned my first haiku. Maybe it stuck with me because somewhere in the forbidden area of my psyche, I'm still crushing on my fifth-grade teacher."

Terrance snickered, his smile tweaking the contours of his countenance into a classic baby face. "What was her name?"

Xander hesitated. "His name."

Terrance cocked his head at the dashboard. "You're gay? But I've seen you with women."

"Technically, I'm bi. But don't worry, I'm not into you." He smirked.

Terrance shrugged. "Not worried." A beat later, he turned to Xander with mock outrage. "But I have to know. Is it because I'm Black?" Xander shook his head. "Because of my glasses?" Xander shook his head again. "I know— I'm too buff. That's it, right?"

"No, man, I just don't like blondes." Xander chortled.

"Hmm. And I'm guessing your dad doesn't know you're bisexual?"

"Correct assumption."

"Your sisters?"

Xander shook his head. "Telling them would be tantamount to telling my dad."

Terrance nodded. "Now that I've met your old man, I can see why you're keeping it quiet."

"I will tell him someday," Xander said solemnly. "It's damaging to one's soul to live a lie."

Terrance sighed. "It could be worse, you know. You

could be a Black gay man. Talk about disenfranchised."

"Right. Of course. What about a Black, gay, trans man? Wouldn't that be the ultimate outsider?" he asked, a hint of his joking tone back.

"I can't even imagine." Terrance frowned. "Being gay and Black would be enough of a burden. My best friend was gay and didn't try to hide it. But he paid the price."

Xander's eyes locked on Terrance's face. "What happened?"

"He got beat up a bunch of times for being gay, by white guys and Black guys. By strangers and by supposed friends. It was a shitty life for him. But he was committed to being who he was. You had to admire him for that."

"Hm. Where is he now?"

Terrance looked out the driver's side window. "That's also a story for another day."

Xander showed no sign of leaving so Terrance flicked his hand toward the passenger door. "Can you get out so I can go home and have a break before I have to see your sorry ass at work in a few hours?"

Xander smiled and exited the vehicle, already mentally in his apartment rolling a decompression joint between his fingers.

DINNER #2

Xander and Sunny walked along the side of the house and swung open the chain-link gate to Xander's childhood backyard.

Kathy, popping neon in a multi-colored shirt and pink pedal pushers, stood sprightly. Jim opened his beer can, bits of foam speckling his unyieldingly wrinkle-free, navy-blue polo shirt, and rose from his patio chair.

"Alex, how are you?" Kathy asked with an awkward hug.

"Phlegmatic, I hope. You?"

Kathy held her bracelet-bedecked arms out to Sunny, beckoning unnecessarily because Sunny insisted on hugging everyone they met and would have initiated had Kathy not done so. "Sunny, so nice to meet you!"

"I brought this for you," Sunny said once disengaged, holding out a small gift bag decorated with signs of the zodiac.

"You shouldn't have!" Kathy extracted a candle, sniffed it heartily and closed her eyes in approval.

"It's a soy candle so it burns cleaner and doesn't have

any petroleum-based ingredients. The vanilla and sandalwood scents create an atmosphere of relaxation and serenity," Sunny said in their mellifluous tone.

"I love it," Kathy said as Xander and Jim shrugged at each other to signal their indifference or possibly skepticism at the candle's capabilities.

"Well, sit down, sit down," Jim said, after a forced hug with Sunny. "We thought we'd enjoy the beautiful day before we start cooking." He smiled, to his son's amazement.

"You're in an unexpectedly jolly mood today," Xander said, immediately regretting the inclusion of 'unexpectedly' in his comment.

"I got a big fat bonus at work yesterday, the sun is shining and my only son is here to visit. What's not to be happy about?" He opened the cooler at his feet and invited Xander and Sunny to dig in.

Xander chose a light beer and lifted the can to Sunny as proof of his willingness to be sociable and accommodating—a goal they'd agreed upon while driving over. He handed Sunny a wine spritzer, the only other option, and downed half his beer in two gulps.

"So, are you two dating?" Kathy asked.

Sunny and Xander laughed, making the older couple exchange confused looks. Xander grabbed Sunny's hand and gave his friend a look that said *Just go with it.* "Sunny is the most amazing person I know, and we have a very special relationship."

Kathy nodded as if that explained everything.

"Tell me, where did you have your first date? I love first date stories."

Sunny and Xander laughed again, making Kathy's smile

fade.

Sunny touched Kathy's arm. "We're only laughing because people don't really date anymore. We all hang out in groups and sometimes, if it's meant to be, we connect in a meaningful way."

"Hmm," Kathy murmured. She glanced around, reached out and touched the top of Sunny's head, pressing down on their short Afro several times. "I just love Black hair. It's so springy. I never get to work with it at the salon." Xander cleared his throat and Kathy yanked her hand back. "And I love your necklace!" she said. "What kind of stones are those?"

Sunny fingered the pendant of seven stacked stones on a leather thong around their neck. "It's got jasper, agate, citrine, lapis lazuli, amethyst and I forget what else. Each stone represents one of the seven chakras or energy centers in the body, which are central to our ability to live a good life, physically, emotionally and spiritually."

"Well, it's very pretty," Kathy said, tucking a stray hair escaped from her updo into submission behind her ear.

Xander popped open a second beer and took a long swig. "By the way, I should inform you that Sunny is non-binary and prefers to go by 'they' instead of 'she'."

"She what?" Jim asked.

"She wants to be called 'they' like there's two of her?" Kathy asked.

Sunny shook their head at Xander, inhaled deeply and smiled with effort at Kathy.

"Don't worry, Mrs. Wallace, I don't have multiple personalities or anything." Sunny laughed lightly. Kathy attempted to laugh too but emitted an odd, strangled sound. "What Xander means is, I don't identify with either the female or male gender."

"So, you're not a woman?" Kathy tilted her head. "You dress like one."

"I wear what feels right to me, which is generally what people consider women's clothing. But I prefer to think of myself as neither sex. I'm just me. I just am."

Jim snorted. "Do you have female body parts or don't you?"

Kathy's mouth dropped open as she slapped Jim's arm.

Jim shrugged. "It's a simple question. If you're born with girl parts, you're female. If you're born with boy parts, you're male." He glared, not at Sunny but at his son as if Sunny's unconventional gender identity were his fault. Or, Xander thought, his father might be neutralizing the temptation to analyze Sunny's body from chest to crotch. "I paid attention that day in high school biology," he sneered.

"You don't have to ans—"

"It's okay, Xan," Sunny said mildly, putting a cinnamon-toned hand on his tan arm. "The parts I was born with are my business, Mr. Wallace. What matters is that today, I prefer not to be thought of as male or female." She turned back to Kathy, clearly the more receptive audience.

"But if you're not male or female, not to be rude but…do you like men or women?" Kathy asked, round-eyed.

"That's a completely different thing, but to answer your question, I like both," Sunny said with an easy smile.

"Could have seen that one coming," Jim said, his head down, hand rubbing his brow.

"Sunny is attracted to all genders including cisgender men and women, transgender men and women, and agender and gender nonconforming individuals," Xander rattled off.

"It's called being 'pansexual'."

"'Pansexual'? I've never heard of that," Kathy said. "What does it mean?"

"It means she'll do it with anybody or anything including probably pots and pans." Jim smirked into his lap.

"Funny. I've never heard that one before." Sunny kept a lilt in their voice that Xander knew required some effort. "Would you like me to explain how people today define how they love?" they asked Kathy, like a teacher preparing her lesson.

"Sure," Kathy said, drawing out the word. Jim said nothing.

"We still have regular heterosexuals—men who love women and women who love men."

"Thank God for small favors," Jim said, staring off into the next yard, probably afraid a neighbor might be in earshot of the conversation, Xander thought.

"Then we have homosexuals which includes gays and lesbians—men who like men, women who like women. We've got bisexuals—people who like both men and women and sometimes other genders."

"What other genders are there? You mean like transsexuals, is that what they're called?" Kathy bounced in her seat like a student who had asked the teacher the desired question. Xander found her eagerness surprising and entertaining.

"Today, they're called transgender people or simply trans."

Jim shrank in his chair as if hoping the conversation wouldn't find him.

Kathy swirled her wine cooler bottle. "You're obviously a lovely person, Sunny, but I have to admit, sometimes it feels like young people are looking for attention with all of these crazy labels. It's like people want their own special, new identity to make them stand out."

"Is that so deplorable? Wanting to be unique?" Xander said.

"I guess not," Kathy said reluctantly. "But in our day, we had regular men, regular women and David Bowie. That was it. And that was plenty."

"This doesn't need to be complicated, Mrs. Wallace. People come in many shapes and sizes. As you're happily married, it shouldn't matter to you what someone else's sexual orientation is anyway."

Jim stood. "I'm gonna get the burgers."

Kathy nodded absently as he entered the house, still looking at Sunny. "Can I ask a question? Hopefully it's not too personal. How can you be attracted to more than one gender? Doesn't one feel right and one feel wrong?"

"Kathy," Sunny said, leaning forward and positioning their hands on their knees. Kathy instinctively leaned toward Sunny as if preparing to hear a secret. "Does a pickle taste the same to you as a doughnut?"

Xander suppressed a laugh from his ringside seat.

"Of course not," Kathy said.

"Do you like them both?"

"I prefer doughnuts, to be honest. I have a sweet tooth," she confessed as Xander grinned. Sunny's eyes flicked to Xander and back while they maintained a straight face.

"Perfect. Some people like the taste of pickles, some prefer doughnuts. I happen to like both. I might even like a pickle-flavored doughnut if one existed. It doesn't make me weird. It means I have broader tastes than some people."

Kathy's face twisted in puzzlement, her circuits visibly

on overload. "Well," she said, standing and brushing imaginary specks off her shorts, "I'm going to bring out the food and we'll get this cookout going."

As she disappeared inside, Xander stood to kiss Sunny on the head. "You're incomparable, Sunny Winston. But you know that."

"We should help bring the food out."

"No, don't. They probably need a minute to decompress. We'll do the cleaning up after we eat." Xander sat back down, stretched out his long legs and wiggled his Teva-clad feet. Sunny curled their legs up underneath them and closed their eyes, their peaceful visage bringing to Xander's mind the image of a benevolent sphinx.

Twenty minutes later, they dug into hamburgers and veggie burgers at the patio table.

"Sunny," Jim said, speaking for the first time since he started grilling the meat. "What do you do for work?" His eyes pleaded for this subject to be innocuous. Xander almost felt badly for continually pulling his dad out of his comfort zone.

"I sell solar energy systems."

Jim grunted. "You've got the name for it."

"Yes, I know!"

"And the disposition," Xander added.

"Someone down the street has solar panels on their house. They don't look that bad," Kathy said.

"I think they're beautiful," Sunny said. "They blend right into dark roofs, plus they prevent air pollution and contribute to the health of the planet and the people on it."

"They're too expensive," Jim interjected dismissively. "I got a quote once because a guy at work's son is in solar." Xander stared at his father, wide-eyed. "It was going to take almost eight years for the panels to be paid off."

"Jim—may I call you Jim?" Sunny waited for his nod. "Have you made any purchases or investments lately that actually pay for themselves?" Jim shook his head slowly as if being lured into a trap. "Everyone knows a new car loses twenty percent of its value in the first year." Jim nodded once. "That's money spent that you'll never get back. So isn't getting paid back over eight years better than not being paid back at all?"

"When you put it that way—"

"Right?" Sunny beamed. "When you're ready for a new quote, you let me know. I'll fix you up with the best deal out there."

Jim turned to his son. "Got a smart one here, don't you?" To Xander's relief, the words were uttered with admiration, not annoyance. He knew if anyone could win over his crusty dad, it was Sunny. He should have brought them home ages ago.

***

Kathy took Sunny inside for a tour after lunch. The house exhaled cool darkness after the heated backyard.

"That's Alex in his Little League uniform." She nodded at the framed five-by-seven Sunny had picked up from an end table next to a tweedy brown couch.

Sunny peered at the boy in his pinstriped outfit and the smiling, proud man with a hand on the boy's shoulder. "He looks mischievous. That fits. And that's Jim?"

"Oh, yes. Jim hardly ever missed a game. I wasn't with him in those days. Emma was still alive. But all of us in the neighborhood had one reason or another to go to the Little League games. I helped out at the snack shack. I don't think Jim ever missed a game."

"Hmm, that must have meant a lot to Xander." Sunny replaced the photo on the table.

Kathy shrugged. "Maybe. He and his father—they don't see eye to eye on a lot of things." Sunny nodded. "I don't know why. I think Jim is just too practical for Xander. And Xander is too—" She paused.

"Too idealistic?" Sunny offered. Kathy nodded. "He is incredibly passionate about saving the world and treating everyone equally and fairly. But so am I. So are a lot of people in our generation. That's not wrong, is it?"

"I guess not." Kathy grasped Sunny's hand and squeezed. "I'm so glad you came. We love it when Alex brings a guest. Our meals are so small since Katie moved away. Let me show you the rest of the house."

***

Outside, amidst the lingering charred beef smoke and light beer sourness, Xander and his father struggled to make conversation, the safest topics already covered while they ate. Xander decided to poke the bear again. See how far he could bring his father along before coming out to him.

"Dad, not to make you uncomfortable, but what do you think about Sunny's attraction to men and women? Do you think it abnormally bizarre or can you understand a tad how someone might love someone else of the same sex?" He fiddled with the tab on top of his beer can.

"What do I think? I'd rather not think about it at all. She seems great, but come on, Alex. If you guys are dating, how do you feel knowing she's been with other women and transsexuals and who knows what? That's worse than being gay and gay is weird enough. Men loving men just isn't natural."

"But it is, actually." Xander spoke evenly and

dispassionately to keep the barbed wire of tension strung between them as slack as possible. "Homosexual relations are, in fact, antediluvian. Cave paintings depict homosexual relationships thousands of years Before Christ. Archaeologists have uncovered similar images all over Europe and Africa, from the earliest civilizations. It's well-known men in ancient Greece had lifelong relationships with each other. And this was all B.C.," Xander said.

"Maybe the coming of Christ shamed them straight," Jim muttered.

"No, actually the trend continued A.C. Emperor Nero of Rome married two men, Pythagoras and Sporus. How about that?"

"Polygamy? That's bad," Jim said in a tsking tone that gave Xander the astonishing impression his father had made a joke.

"The buried city of Pompeii revealed artwork showing men copulating with men and women with women. And we haven't even left the first century yet."

"Okay, you can stop the history lesson. I get it. It's been around a long time."

Xander held his breath, savoring the ground he'd gained. A rewarding breeze lifted his bangs.

"But that doesn't mean they need to broadcast it, marching around in skimpy outfits, demanding to be treated equally at the same time they want everyone to notice how different they are." Xander's moment of effervescence fizzled out. "I don't wanna know who people vote for. I don't wanna know how much money they make. And I don't wanna know who they're sleeping with. Why can't we all just live our lives and not bother each other?"

"Because, Dad, gay people are still discriminated against

in our contumelious society." The edge he'd kept at bay as long as possible latched onto his voice like iron filings on a magnet. He ignored the voice in the back of his head reminding him Jim's words weren't a personal attack. They couldn't be. "They're still denied some of the rights straight people take for granted."

"They got gay marriage, didn't they? What else do they need? Sometimes it seems like people just like the fight." Jim stood. "Well, thanks for stopping by. That Sunny's an interesting one. Not shy, is she?"

"How do you feel about me and Sunny dating, them being Black and all?"

"Jesus, you can't stop, can you? It's like you keep picking at a scab, making it worse. I don't care about her skin color. There. Happy?" The harsh sun spotlighted spittle leaping from Jim's lips.

He stomped into the house.

DINNER #3

The generally unflappable Xander lost sleep and appetite in the days leading up to dinner with his father and stepmother. *I'm going to come out to my dad.* No matter how many times he repeated this simple statement, in his head or out loud, it refused to budge from the world of the abstract into a concrete plan.

Much as he wanted to blame his friends for this, he knew it was his choice and his alone. And he was as ready to try as he'd ever be.

He'd been lazing around the firepit at Buwan's family's summer home last weekend with the gang as the stars and the crickets woke up. While Buwan refilled wine glasses for the group of new and old friends, Xander noticed with suspicion that Sunny and Jess were whispering, heads close together.

"It's never good when those two start plotting something," Xander mumbled to Terrance. He dropped his hand to stroke his black-and-white mutt Fred, who lay at his side.

"Xander," Sunny finally said, reaching forward and taking his hand. The light from the flames caressed their tawny face. "Honey. Terrance and I were talking earlier about the difficult relationship you have with your dad."

Xander tossed a pained look Terrance's way but his friend's attention rested wholly on cleaning his glasses.

"Your friends who love you so much wonder if you're ready to be honest with your family about being bisexual. You know we would never pressure you. It's completely up to you. But you say you want to tell them, so we hate seeing you tortured by this secret. Maybe opening up will actually improve things with your dad. Or at least let you feel more like yourself when you're around him."

The wind shifted the fire's direction, moving shadows across Xander's eyes. "Not happening. He's not ready to know."

Jess poked a stick in the fire, her asymmetrical brown hair swinging with the movement. "X, he may never be ready. But you can't keep this inside forever. Don't you agree it's time? Your friends all know."

Xander sighed. "I don't know why you guys should care if I reveal myself to him or not."

"A good friend of mine—that would be you—told me it's damaging to one's soul to live a lie," Terrance said. "But it's totally up to you. Maybe it would help if you explained why you don't want to come out to your dad. If you want."

Buwan laughed at Terrance. "Did anyone ever say you should have been a therapist? You ask 'why' more than a four-year-old." He turned to Xander. "Some things are hard to explain. I get it. And it's not really any of our business."

Xander ruffled Fred's fur for a minute. Something had to give in his relationship with his dad. That was evident. A reset would be welcome.

Just as Jess started to change the subject, he spoke. "Maybe you're right. He may never be receptive to the truth. But perhaps I am ready to introduce him to the real me." He leaned over and cocked his head at Fred who replied with a kiss on Xander's nose. "If I do it, will one of you go with, to back me up if needed?"

"No way," said Terrance, grinning widely. "Still recovering from the last dinner."

Sunny gently poked Xander's arm with a maternal smile. "Same."

Xander looked at the other three.

Charley swallowed. "I could go?"

"No," Sunny said with a head shake. "That's not fair to Charley. Jess could do it."

Jess sighed long and loudly. "Sure, Xander." Xander knew her use of his full name instead of the succinct "X" she preferred was intended to convey the magnitude of her sacrifice. "I've heard the horror stories from Sunny and Terrance but if it makes it easier for you, I'll come."

"She says as if giving up her firstborn," Sunny joked.

"Bless you, Jessica," Xander said, bowing with prayer hands.

Jess scoffed. "Since you're a humanist, I'm not sure how much weight that carries. But blessing accepted all the same." She smiled and poked the fire again.

Now, as he sat shotgun in Jess's used BMW, his entire being throbbed with dread as if being forced to present to the sixth-grade class on a book he forgot to read. But ten times worse. He'd been hoping this momentous occasion would resemble the most challenging mountain climb he'd ever undertaken: the path to the summit reeking of hardship but the rush of fulfillment at the peak delivering sweet triumph and inner peace, making the journey worth it. He would be a different person—a better one—afterward.

Yet every time he envisioned the scene, he pictured himself handing over a piece of his soul on a silver platter for his father to ridicule and, ultimately, reject. He might as well lop off his head and plop that on the platter too.

In another strange occurrence, Xander found himself at a loss for words. The daily semantic choices he made for sheer pleasure were frivolous in comparison to tonight's linguistic challenge, when how he said it seemed as critical as what he said. Improper choices might extirpate their entire fragile relationship, such as it was.

Which words would provoke the least? Which words would encourage understanding and acceptance? Did such words even exist in the universe? If so, he hadn't yet found them he despaired, as Jess pulled into the driveway of the triple-decker.

Jess killed the engine. "You okay?"

Xander's head made repeated, tiny bobs. "Sure. It's merely another dinner with my dad, right?"

She patted his jean-clad leg and got out of the car.

***

Kathy turned to Jess as they tucked into steaming plates of spaghetti and meatballs, Texas toast on the side. "You've got a beautiful tan. Do you go to a tanning salon?"

Resisting the urge to fib and end the conversation, like she normally would, Jess decided to be honest, setting a tone for the night and encouraging Xander to do the same. "No, this is my normal color."

"You Mexican? Puerto Rican?" Jim asked.

"I'm American, born and raised here. But my parents are

from Colombia, hence the year-round tan." She smiled confidently.

"Colombia?" Kathy asked. "Like the coffee growers I see on the TV ads?"

"Well, yes," Jess said, picturing her hosts picturing an old man with a huge mustache leading a basket-laden burro through a coffee plantation. "That's the same country and Colombia is known for its coffee. But my family aren't farmers. My father is a lawyer and my mother runs a dental office."

"Hmm." Jim's undefinable reaction silenced Jess.

"Do you by chance watch *Modern Family*?" Xander contributed, which Jess took as a good sign; he was engaged in the conversation, not brooding like he did the entire drive over. "The actor Sofia Vergara is Colombian. So they export more than coffee."

Jess laughed but cut it short when no one else joined in.

"I know her! She's on the cover of the magazines in the salon all the time! She's so beautiful. But why don't you sound like her?"

Xander sighed and rubbed the small bump on the bridge of his nose. "Born and bred here, Kathy, did you not hear her say that? Jess is American and was born here."

After that brief contribution, Xander visibly shrank back into his thoughts, so Jess took charge of the conversation while he zoned out.

"You're pretty ambitious for your generation," Jim said after Jess told them about her accounting career achievements and goals. "It's good to see a young person who cares about the company they work for. Most people your age just float along, hopping between jobs, no loyalty, trying to find themselves." The last phrase dripped with disdain.

Jess shrugged off the suggestion that her friends were unfocused and accepted the compliment with a slow nod.

"Lazy is what they are," he continued. "Because they got those ridiculous trophies as kids, just for showing up. No one should get a trophy for that."

"It does make the kids expect good things like an award or a treat without having to earn it," Kathy added, in case Jess wasn't clear on Jim's point.

"Entitlement, Kathy, that's what it's called."

Jess smiled, which was taking increasing effort. "You know, sometimes millennials change jobs a lot because we want to be passionate about what we do. Accounting may sound dull, but I love my job. If I didn't, I'd move on because life is too short to toil away at something you don't love. It's that old cliché." She peeked at Xander to see if invoking a cliché got a rise out of him, but he was focused on pushing pasta around his plate with his fork. "We want to work to live, not live to work."

"I've never heard that before. I like it. And I love my job too," Kathy said, as if trying to bond with Jess.

"But my guys at the factory, the younger ones," Jim said, "are so demanding. They all want flexible hours and better benefits."

"Doesn't everyone?" Jess asked with a head tilt and soft smile. "Maybe the difference is that our generation is willing to ask for it."

"One of our office ladies actually asked management to let her work from home." He belched a belly laugh at the ludicrousness of the request. "Can you imagine that? We're a damn factory. Can't really run a production line if half the people work somewhere else." He sat back, grinning, as if he'd single-handedly debunked the entire concept of telecommuting.

He seemed to take Jess's silence as agreement and forged on. "And so many of you people take the feel-good job instead of the one that's best for their family." He stared at Xander, his mouth twitching.

Jess placed her fork next to her butter knife, in perfect alignment. "Millennials and the generations after us were brought up to give back, to do good. We're more socially engaged. So a job choice that seems selfish to one person might seem noble and generous to someone else." She noticed Xander completely missed her skillful defense of his career.

"How are you socially engaged?" Kathy asked with a touch of trepidation as if she were asking about a social disease. Jim glared at her, Jess assumed for taking the conversation in a direction he didn't care about.

"Well, a bunch of us went to a rally a few weeks ago to protest racial profiling in the city's police department, and—"

A half-laugh-half-groan burst from Jim's chest. "So let me guess. You probably sympathize with the Blacks who complain about being stopped by the police, even though they commit more crimes? And while we're at it, why don't we coddle the illegal aliens flooding across the border?"

Jess's dark brown eyes flinched. Not wanting the conversation to take a controversial turn before Xander's big announcement, she chose to address the conflict for which she and Jim shared common ground.

"Oh no, I'm against illegal immigration. You wouldn't believe how much it costs us taxpayers."

Jim rubbed his chin with a meaty hand. "Exactly." He

looked at Xander again. "It's a scourge on our society. I wish they would all stay home. You don't see us rushing their borders."

Jess narrowed her eyes, debating a measured response, but Kathy cut in.

"I heard there's a Women's March this weekend."

"Yeah, a bunch of us are actually going," Jess said.

Jim shook his head. "People who protest should worry about their own families instead of sticking their noses in other people's business."

"I'm thinking I might go," Kathy said. "Sally and Linda invited me to go with them."

Jim's face contorted.

"Just to see what the fuss is about," she added with downcast eyes.

Jess pondered how to move the talk onto safer ground but decided she had lost control of the conversation. In fact, based on the darkening storm cloud on Jim's face, Kathy's news threatened to derail the entire night. It was now or never.

"So Xander, isn't there something you want to tell your father?"

Xander's face blanched and twisted as if his stomach were threatening to return his spaghetti to the table in unceremonious fashion. He stared at the white strands squiggling through the heavy red sauce on his plate.

"Dad, I—I—well—"

"Spit it out, son."

Xander raised his head. "I'm dating Jess."

Jim's face budged not a smidge.

"That's wonderful," Kathy said, "isn't it, Jim? But what about—" Kathy stopped herself. "Sunny?" she whispered as if Jess wouldn't hear.

Xander tossed his head like a high-strung horse. "Oh. Sunny and I were never really dating." Jess raised her eyebrows at him. He ignored her. She wrinkled her nose and pursed her lips. She placed a hand on his arm.

"Aw, that's sweet of you to say, but let's be honest, Xan." She faced Jim. "We're just really, really, old, good friends. Xander hasn't found his one true love yet." She nudged Xander's foot with hers under the table. His face behind the beard looked sickly—pale and sunken, deprived of its usual vitality. He stared at his plate again with unseeing eyes. Try as she might, she couldn't see him breathing—no rise and fall of his chest or shoulders.

Jess reached for his hand under the table and squeezed. "Kathy. Jim. Thank you so much for dinner. The food was great. Would it be rude if we made an early exit? I have to be at work at seven tomorrow morning."

Xander flew from the house like a thoroughbred released from the starting gate.

***

Sunny led Xander a few steps away from their cluster of friends after the Women's March that weekend. "Do you want to tell me what happened at your dad's house?" they said softly. "Are you ready to talk about it?"

Xander's blue eyes lurked about as if seeking safe harbor. "Sunny, you know better than anyone, you can't force this."

They took his hand. "I know. I only want you to tell me what's going on with you. Where your head is at."

"I couldn't do it. It's as simple as that. The thought made me legit nauseous."

Sunny nodded and waited.

"I guess someone who's got a decent relationship with

his parents takes less of a risk in coming out. Their opinion of their son might slip a little or it might stay the same. But when you consider my dad's already low opinion of me, why did I think for a nanosecond that my coming out to him would be beneficial, for either of us?"

"Hm. You know you can't control his reaction and you can't control his opinion of you."

"But in his eyes, I'll be even less of a person—even more unlike the kind he wants me to be."

"Xander Wallace. Look at me." They waited until his cobalt gaze landed on them. "Don't you ever say anything like that again. You are a good person. No, you are an outstanding person. You have more empathy and caring in your pinkie finger than most people have in their entire bodies. Your dad sees you through his own lens and maybe that lens is distorted or grimy. He doesn't see all of you. That doesn't make you any less of a person."

Xander pulled his hand away and slumped to the extent his standing position allowed, eyes downcast. "That's easy for you to say with the world's most progressive parents, who cherish you unequivocally. That's why it wasn't a big deal when you came out."

Sunny stared at Xander. "Who said it wasn't a big deal?"

"You told me you disclosed you were pan one day and they said okay, thanks for telling us, and that was that."

"That's what happened. But that doesn't mean it was easy for me to decide to tell them, or to get the words out when the time came. I didn't dare admit who I was for years. The bullying didn't help. I've been called bull dyke, freak and—my favorite—oompah lesbo," they said with uncharacteristic snideness and a glance at their orange-brown arm. "The bullies made me want to go underground and stay there. So like most of us non-hetero types, I did a lot of soul-searching before I decided it was best for me to be honest about who I was." They rolled their shoulders back. "You helped me a lot with that, you know."

"Me? I thought you were completely out and well-adjusted when I met you."

Sunny sighed. "That's my curse in life—everyone thinks I'm always happy and content and well-adjusted. When we became friends in college, it was like I had permission to be one-hundred-percent me for the first time in my life. You brought that out in me."

Xander smiled sadly and stroked the side of their face. Sunny grabbed his hand again and held it tightly.

"Look, I know how hard it is to find those words and to say them. It's like tearing open your chest and exposing your naked heart to the outside world. An unkind outside world. Just remember, if you do this, you're not coming out for him. And it's not about improving your relationship with him. His reaction doesn't even matter. It's all for you, love." They kissed his hand. "I have an idea. I think you need to stop worrying about coming out to your dad and enjoy being bi. Be proud of your sexuality again. Let's work on that."

"What do you propose?"

"Let's get more active in the city's LGBTQ scene. You've never even come to a meeting with me."

"Deal." Xander pulled Sunny into a hug and buried his face in their velvety neck. The strings of their beaded headband tickled his nose.

DINNER #4

ander's excitement bubbled out of him, making Charley picture how adorable he must have been as a boy. She conjured up a four-year-old in red plaid flannel pajamas staring at a Christmas tree sheltering scads of gifts, mouth open wide, eyes open wider.

"Dad's going to be ecstatic. I cannot wait to see his face when I present you."

Charley turned off the ignition and squinted at him in the passenger seat. "Why, exactly?"

"You're white as can be and comely and normal," he replied as if the answer were obvious. "And our friendship has progressed to dating. Officially dating," he smirked. "That should compensate for me missing last month's dinner."

Unsure how she felt about being held up as the epitome of normalcy, and trying to ignore the surety that normal translated to boring, her squint deepened, pulling in her brow. She stared through the windshield at the tan house.

"By the way, Char, are you religious? It's not as high on

Dad's list of hot buttons as race and immigration but it comes up on occasion."

"Not really," she said, because that's what she thought he wanted to hear. "I stopped going to church a long time ago." A tiny voice in the back of her head reprimanded her for not telling the whole story—how she'd not given up on God but remained in limbo since her parents and grandparents died, trying to figure out how to relate to her. God being God, she hoped God would drop the answer into her lap someday.

"Hm. Better to avoid that topic, then. He's touchy about people who don't believe in God."

Charley chose not to point out those weren't her words. She clutched his strong hand. "Come on, let's try to make this fun."

Xander stroked her long, light brown hair, kissed her hand and got out of the car.

Kathy gushed over Charley like a new puppy at first, making Charley feel awkward and embarrassed. Jim seemed okay, if a little loud and opinionated. He made one snide comment about Xander's job when Xander announced his big win that stopped Liam Flammer's project. But he was far from the two-headed monster she expected. Xander seemed content to sit back, smiling, and let the three of them carry the conversation.

"Alex," Kathy said as Jim helped himself to seconds on pot roast, "guess what I did?" She glanced at Jim, then back to Xander. "I went to a protest—that Women's March— with my girlfriends." Charley picked up a note of beseeching as if Kathy sought her stepson's approval. Xander didn't respond and Jim's head was buried in his plate, so Charley did.

"That's so cool, Kathy. Did you like it?"

"I did!" Kathy enthused. "I never thought much about fighting for a cause. I think a lot of us accept whatever life dishes out. But it made me feel so. . . .strong? Happy?" She shook her head and laughed.

"Empowered. Is that what you felt?" Charley asked.

"Yes. That's it. Empowered." Kathy's eyes shone.

"I know what you mean. I only went to my first protest a while ago, after meeting Xander." Charley beamed at him but her smile faded at his blank face. She turned back to Kathy. "It's such a simple concept—join a group to say something's wrong—but so many of us never even think about doing it. I see the world in a whole new way now." She stopped, embarrassed by her babbling and her relatively feeble commitment compared to her boyfriend's.

Jim stared at the fork making trips back and forth from his plate to his mouth. Xander's eyes alternated between his dad and the far wall.

"Xan." Charley nudged his arm. "Isn't that great that Kathy went to her first protest?"

Xander looked at Charley and then Kathy. "Sure, one has to start somewhere. But to make a material difference, you must do more than merely show up."

Kathy smiled uncertainly. "What do you mean?"

Xander closed his eyes and intoned: *"Donate to the cause. Write letters to media. Call legislators."*

He opened his eyes and smiled at Charley before turning to Kathy.

"Most of all, keep showing up. To march, to volunteer, to be seen and heard."

Kathy nodded.

"Our last protest," Charley said, to draw the focus off

Kathy, "was the candlelight vigil for Jamal Taylor, the teenager shot by the police."

Jim's piercing eyes found Charley. Her hand flew to her silver nose ring, then slid down to the mole under her lip, which she rubbed with her thumb. "That the Black kid who went after the officer with a switchblade?"

"Dad, he didn't brandish a knife," Xander said with more impatience than Charley thought necessary. She dropped her hand from her lip and watched. "He didn't even have one. It was a racially motivated, aggravated assault by the police, no debate about it. And the Mayor is a travesty on two legs. For all his effluence, he's done nothing about Jamal Taylor just like he's done nothing about rampant profiling in the police department."

Kathy's eyebrows knitted together. "But if he had a knife, it wouldn't have mattered what color skin he had, would it?" She turned to Charley. "I don't see Black or white. I tell myself we're all the same."

"He didn't ha—" Xander stopped. He flashed Charley a wry smile, his expression suggesting they two alone grasped reality. Although feeling a touch sorry for Kathy, Charley thrilled at their unspoken connection. She wasn't like Kathy. Her activism had evolved and she existed on a higher plane now, one in Xander's stratosphere.

"Charley, can I ask you a personal question?" Kathy said. A subtle groan escaped Jim's chest. He immediately reached for the bowl of boiled potatoes as if to tie the two actions together. "Did you grow up with African-Americans and other races, or was your town all white?"

"Well, as a kid I lived in a mostly white suburb, but in high school, I lived here in the city with kids of all races."

"And would you say you see color because of that, or

that you don't see color because of that?"

Xander and Jim both eyed Kathy with surprise.

Charley twirled her fork a few times before putting it down. "Both, I guess. I definitely became more aware of different races during high school. And I felt like an outsider sometimes. But I also made some great friends on the cross-country team including a Black girl and an Asian boy. So in the end, it made me see color, but also realize that it doesn't matter."

"To you," Xander said. "Color doesn't matter to you. But you don't discount the importance of race or pretend it has no bearing on the thought processes and behaviors of many people."

Charley nodded rather than admit her thinking hadn't progressed to that level of sophistication.

"You can't simply pronounce that color doesn't matter," he said to Kathy as if weary of his own voice pointing out the same issues again. "It's not adequate to not be racist. Doing nothing means you condone the behavior. You have to be decidedly anti-racist. You have to speak up when you witness racist behavior."

Jim let loose with a huge sigh, but Kathy hung on Xander's words and nodded when he finished. "I admit I've turned my head or shut my mouth when a friend said something mean about a minority person. Next time, I'll try to say something."

Xander smiled at her, making Charley want to thank him for cutting his stepmother some slack. "That would be commendable, Kathy. Remember, you have the power to help change the world for the better."

The surprised and slightly proud look Kathy gave Xander made Charley think this was the first time the two of them ever related in a meaningful way. Jim also glanced from one to the other, his look impossible to decipher.

***

"Dinner went well, don't you think?" Charley snuggled on Xander's couch, the TV set to a news station, Fred on the floor at Xander's feet. Jess was on a date and his other roommate was out, so they had the apartment to themselves. "Did you get what you wanted?"

Xander cocked his head as if the concept were new to him. He turned the TV volume down to a murmur. "I guess if my desire was a relatively peaceful meal, then yes—I got what I wanted."

"But. . . ."

"If I sought some kind of bonding with my dad, even a tenuous one, then I didn't."

"Hmm. What *do* you want from your dad, Xan?"

Xander rested his hand on Charley's thigh and stroked it with his thumb. The tails of his woven bracelets wiggled. "I guess the ultimate would be for him to sanction my career choice and accept me for who I am, including my sexuality. But that's unlikely. He'll never move further along the spectrum of empathy and understanding."

"Have you ever talked to him about your mother's death?"

Xander's hand stilled. He shifted to face Charley. "What's that got to do with anything?"

Charley shrugged. "It seems like maybe you have to deal with the elephant in the room before you can move on to other things. You've got this shared demon in your past that no one's talking about."

Xander's blue eyes studied her for so long she dropped her eyes momentarily.

"We've had years in which to talk about it so it's reasonably safe to assume no one wants to. He's never asked how I felt. Not once."

This time, he looked away from her steady gaze.

Charley pulled up her legs and settled into a cross-legged position, facing Xander. She released her long hair from the clip she'd stuck in when they got to the apartment, and tousled her long tresses the way he liked. She took his hand.

"You know, when my parents died, I never thought about how it affected my grandparents. One day, cross-country practice was canceled so I got home early and I heard Gram in her bedroom, bawling her eyes out. I was too afraid to talk to her, so I snuck out and wandered around the neighborhood for an hour. I think she may have known, because that night, Gramps and I had a talk. We liked to sit on our little porch and it was a hot night, so we're out there under the moon and he starts talking about Mom."

"Charley," Gramps had said as they sat side by side on the wicker porch swing, "I know you miss your mom and dad. You must know Edith and I miss them too."

His direct approach scared Charley a little. "I know," she'd said quietly.

"Jane was our little girl, and a part of who we are, so when we lost her, it left a gaping hole. Don't worry if you catch one of us grieving. It's all normal."

Charley's face reddened as if she'd been caught spying on Gram.

"But now we have you," Phil said, patting her hand. "And you're helping make us whole again."

Fear shot through Charley like an arrow through yielding flesh. Her throat tightened at the prospect of being responsible for her grandparents' wholeness.

Phil stopped patting but left his weighty palm on top of her hand. "I'm not telling you this to upset you. We are each responsible for our own happiness."

***

Charley let go of Xander's hand and changed the cross of her legs since her left foot was about to fall asleep. Fred lifted his head from his paws to watch before settling back down with a sigh. "I didn't understand what he meant for a long time."

"But you do now?" Xander asked.

"I think so. He was telling me their sadness was not my burden."

"I wish I'd known your Gramps."

"Me too." She cleared her throat. "But there's a point to my story. Death changes everyone. At fifteen, I was too selfish to see their pain—"

"I beg to differ," Xander interrupted. "You were human and young and in pain yourself."

"Okay. But I feel like people spend a lot of time and energy trying to make sense of death. But we do it alone. It's weird and sad that when a family should pull together, sometimes we push each other away."

Her pointed look confirmed she spoke of his family now, not hers.

"It takes two to tango." He spoke with soft disdain.

Charley knew now was not the time to point out he'd uttered a cliché. She sighed. Maybe she couldn't help with this. "I just don't think you should waste a parent unless it's truly a lost cause."

Xander's upper body wavered back and forth as if blown by an unexpected breeze.

"Maybe it is," he said glumly.

"Then why, Xander, do you keep going back?"

He startled, and turned back to face the TV.

"Wait," she said, taking the remote from his hand. "I want to say something else." Xander looked at her with sad eyes. "I don't think you're desperate for your father's approval. I think you're desperate for his love. I feel guilty because I'm not sure I loved my parents enough when they were here. And I feel sad because I'm not sure they loved me enough."

"You have to stop concerning yourself with that. What we have has to be enough."

"I know. But what if you don't know how much you have? And you can still find out?"

DINNER #5

Their visit was short—barely long enough to drink two beers and eat half a meal. In hindsight, maybe Xander should have said no to Buwan when they found themselves with thirty extra minutes, the subway having been refreshingly quick, and his impish friend suggested they kill a six-pack before heading to Jim's house.

Things started well, Buwan entertaining Kathy with lively, self-deprecating stories about his artistic journey, and carefully chosen bits about his mom and her well-to-do family. Based on pre-dinner warnings, he avoided the fact that he had two mothers. To Xander's amazement and relief, neither Jim nor Kathy interrogated Buwan about the origin of his deep-bronze skin.

Xander's buzz eroded his standard irritation, making him question why he'd never before turned to alcohol to dull the misery of these home visits.

When Kathy asked what the boys were up to after dinner, Buwan answered nonchalantly while cutting his next bite of steak. "We're headed in town for the Black Lives Matter protest."

Jim grunted, right on schedule.

Kathy's eyes widened. "I saw last night's protest on the news. It was scary, how the protestors threatened the police."

Xander's fork stopped halfway to his mouth. He put it down. "Who's more threatening or intimidating, Kathy—an individual armed with nothing but a homemade sign, or a cop sporting a bulletproof vest, helmet and shield? Regardless, we protestors are not trying to scare the police. We're trying to wake them up." He gave his alcohol-loosened tongue free rein. After all, he thought, Kathy's nascent interest in activism deserved nurturing and education. "Plus, the police are already scared. That's why the police and the politicians and all the powers-that-be continue to oppress minorities—out of fear that empowered minorities will take something away from them."

Kathy cocked her head. "Like what?"

"I don't know—whatever matters most to them. Their jobs, their livelihoods, their women, their men, their neighborhoods."

Buwan leaned in. "Their control."

Kathy glanced at Bu and back to Xander. "Do you think tonight's protest will be dangerous?"

Xander shrugged. "It depends on how the cops comport themselves. If they push the crowds or throw teargas or fire rubber bullets, people will fight back."

Jim's face puckered as if he'd swallowed an entire, very tart lime.

"No son of mine better raise a hand toward a cop. I

raised you better than that."

Xander hiccupped. He swallowed a bite of steak and raised his blue eyes to his father. "Did you? Raise me, I mean?"

Jim's napkin dropped to the table. "What the hell is that supposed to mean?"

"Let's be honest, Dad. Mom raised me. Not you. Charley insists we should talk about Mom." He hiccupped again, loudly. "'Cause we never have."

Jim's eyes registered a beat of pain. Kathy shrank into her seat. Bu continued eating, not looking but clearly listening to the father-son exchange.

"This is hardly the time for that."

"Yeah, why rush it? It's only been sixteen years since she died." He smirked at Bu.

"You're out of line, Alex."

"Maybe you're out of line too. Why didn't you let me mourn her?" Xander's voice hitched. "She was my mother!"

Jim stood, a hand steadying his chair before it could topple over.

"It's time for you to go."

He ushered Xander to the front door, Buwan trailing behind.

Xander marched down the front steps and practically ran the first block.

"Congratulations, Buwan Bakunawa, on witnessing my first official, unceremonious eviction from my own home." He slowed his pace, rubbed his right eye and circled his shoulders a few times.

Bu patted Xander's shoulder. "Naw, he didn't kick you out. He suggested you leave."

BREAKFAST

"Alexander Wallace, you've been sprung."

The cop unlocked the holding cell door with a jangle of keys and slid it open with a screech of metal. The other men in the cell uttered "Way to go" and "Peace" as Xander trudged through the door and to a counter where another cop returned his cell phone, wallet and bandana in a large plastic bag.

Freed from his cellmates, Xander recoiled at his own smell—a pungent combination of body odor, dust and fear lingering on his T-shirt and jeans. He'd been careful not to touch his face and spread the tear gas residue, but he had a cough and stinging eyes from his brief, indirect exposure.

In the police station's lobby, Jim leaned against a cinder block wall near the exit, wearing a neat, brown cotton windbreaker and pressed jeans. His graying hair was damp, his face ruddy and freshly shaved.

Steeling himself, Xander walked over and stuck out his hand. "Thanks for bailing me out, Dad. I'll pay you back, obviously. I guess they might drop the charges, so that's good."

Jim grumbled. "At least it's Sunday so I didn't have to leave work to rescue my wayward son." Xander couldn't read the expression on Jim's face. His voice sounded neutral.

"I can take the train home."

"I'm here. I might as well drive you."

A deep cough wracked Xander's body, making his eyes water.

Jim's blue eyes narrowed. "Let's get you out of here." Outside in the morning sun, so bright Xander's eyes watered more, Jim walked to the side of the wide concrete steps leading down to the street. "Sit."

Xander stiffened. He wanted to be home in bed. But he eased himself down beside Jim, every muscle complaining.

"Son, what's going on?"

Xander squeezed his eyes to stop the burning. It didn't help. "The protest got a bit out of hand. The cops started arresting everyone, even if they didn't see you causing mayhem. Buwan got arrested too. Not sure where he ended up—" His voice trailed off. He didn't want to lie and feign complete innocence, but he didn't feel like divulging details of his destructive behavior either. He was disgusted with himself for breaking his code of ethics and vandalizing a police car. No need to pile Jim's disgust on top of that.

"Yeah, I got that. What I want to know is, why? You were such a sweet kid." Xander turned and stared at Jim. "Always helping the other kids, saving every little damn animal. Now it seems like you're angry all the time."

Xander dropped his head.

"You're more like me than you think. Not because you got arrested—that was stupid. But you're a fighter. How do you think I survived fifteen years of living with a man who used me as a punching bag? How do you think I managed to protect my little sister? By taking my licks and getting a very thick skin. I vowed I'd survive if only to prove him wrong—that I wasn't a piece of shit like he said."

Xander kept his head low but his ears alert. He vaguely knew his grandfather was a bastard but didn't know details. Still, what was Jim's point? "So you were cold and hard with me to make me tougher? Really? Thank God I had Mom to balance you out."

Jim emitted a soft groan, like a small animal in pain or fear.

"Maybe you're more like your father than you realize," Xander said. From the corner of his eye, he saw Jim flinch.

"I hope to hell not. When I proposed to your mother, she made me promise I wouldn't repeat the cycle of abuse. She said she wasn't going to live in fear of me turning into my father. I thought I did all right. I never raised a finger to you kids."

Xander cleared his irritated throat. "You spanked me the time I spilled juice on the new rug after Mom told me not to leave the kitchen."

Jim laughed, making Xander look at him with surprise. "I thought Emma was going to spank me for spanking you—she was so mad." His eyes softened at the memory. Xander cocked his head. His dad looked a touch more human when his guard dropped. "Anyway, I can't have you turning out like your grandfather. Tell me that's not what's going on here."

Xander shook his head and met Jim's gaze with his watery, bloodshot eyes. "No, Dad. I'm not feeling violent. I have no predisposition to hurt anyone. I'm just extremely frustrated lately." He planted his elbows on his thighs and rested his heavy head in his hands. His fingers wove through his hair.

"Okay. Tell me. Why the frustration?"

"You do not want to have this conversation, trust me," Xander mumbled.

"Try me. I'm a captive audience."

Xander stared at his sneakers.

"Okay. You're a captive audience. I'm not giving you a ride home until you talk to me."

One of Xander's fingers tapped on his skull a few times. All his fingers came to life, drumming on his scalp.

Sporadic Sunday traffic purred past the police station.

The morning sun found the sliver of neck between his hair and his collar.

He inhaled deeply, his raw throat itching.

"Remember when Kathy said in your day, there were men, women and David Bowie?"

Jim cleared his throat. "No, but go on."

"Well, when it comes to sexual orientation, I'm like David Bowie." Xander continued staring at his feet. Thirty seconds passed. He counted in time with his ragged breaths.

Jim shifted heavily on the concrete step, coming a bit closer and lowering his voice. "So you like guys. You're gay." His voice rose unnaturally on the last word.

"I'm bisexual. I am sexually attracted to both men and women. I don't expect you to condone it."

He waited, half expecting no reply.

"How can I condone something I don't understand?"

Xander was silent.

Jim tried again. "That wasn't rhetorical. Help me understand. Start by telling me when you made this decision.”

Xander’s head shook in his hands. “It’s not a concept you opt for and shape to your liking. It chooses you.” He rubbed his eyes and resumed his position, head in hands. “It’s difficult to explain. We can’t control who we’re attracted to. You can’t imagine being attracted to a man, right?” He took the silence as assent. “Well, I can’t imagine not being attracted to a man. It’s not something I control.”

“But most of the world sees that as wrong. I don’t know how it can feel right.”

Xander sat up straight and wrapped the hanging end of his leather bracelet around his finger. “I don’t see how you marrying Kathy ten months after Mom died could feel right. But I accept it.”

He peeked at his father but quickly withdrew his gaze from the flash of anger in Jim’s eyes.

“So what you’re saying is, you can’t change who you are.”

Xander nodded.

“Then you’ll understand that I can’t change who I am either. Do I understand guys who love guys? No. Does it give me the heebie jeebies to think about? Yeah. But you’re my son.”

Xander waited. The heaviness in his chest tightened, making him wheeze. A soft breeze set his eyes watering and burning again.

Jim shifted on the hard step again. “I love you. You know that.”

Xander silently savored the words.

“So, all the women you said you were dating—were any of those real?”

“Yes. All those women were real. They were not mannequins or blow-up dolls.” Xander smiled at the step between his feet.

Jim guffawed. Xander raised his head. Looked at his dad. And laughed with him.

"And I did go out with Sunny. And Charley—I'm not sure where that stands now though. But not Jess. Never Jess." He shuddered at the thought of he and Jessica romantically involved.

"Well, son, I mean this for real: I hope someday you love someone—anyone—the way I loved your mother."

The pain in Jim's eyes transfixed Xander. He couldn't look away.

"When Emma died, I felt like a huge part of me—all the good parts—got erased. I'd look in the mirror and didn't recognize who I saw. I wasn't the same without her." Now Jim hung his head and stared at his shoes. "I hope you never go through that."

"Why don't you ever talk about her? It's like you expunged her from our lives and we weren't allowed to grieve. You even hijacked all the photos."

Jim raised his head and stared at the traffic—his face now haggard, eyes and jowls drooping. "I couldn't look at the pictures. I guess I should've left them up, but I didn't want you kids to suffer. Like I was suffering. I thought it was better for everyone to move on." He sighed and ran a hand over his graying head.

"I had to hide the one torn photo I had under my mattress, like Mom was contraband."

Jim fidgeted, coins jingling in his pants pocket. "What do you want from me, Alex?"

Xander hesitated, unsure how to take the question. A raspy coughing fit bought him some time. "For starters, can you call me Xander? I know Mom liked Alex but it's not the name that connects us to her. I think she'd welcome me adapting my name to something that fits me better, just like she'd understand my sexual orientation."

Jim's eyes narrowed.

"Okay. Xander."

"And—"

"There's more?"

Xander froze.

"I'm kidding. Keep going."

"Can we talk about Mom on occasion? Maybe trade a story or two?"

Jim's chest rose and fell. "Sure. As long as they're not about the damn trophies."

Xander tensed, then realized Jim was smiling, the corners of his eyes crinkling. The last time he remembered making his dad's eyes crinkle, he'd scored his one and only homerun, at age ten.

"Dad, you have to get over this trophy hang-up. First of all, participation trophies didn't start with my generation. The baby boomers started it. Second of all, research indicates they don't cause any undue harm."

Jim scoffed.

"Plus, I'll tell you a secret." He leaned toward his father. "I never cared about the trophies. They didn't make me feel special at all. But Mom loved them so much, I never had the heart to tell her I thought they were asinine."

Jim leaned back and regarded his son. He nodded, smiled and leaned back in. He wrapped an arm around Xander's shoulder and squeezed.

"What's with the cough and the wheezing? You're not getting asthma like your mother I hope."

Xander shook his head. "It's only a teargas hangover."

Jim stared for a second before looking away.

"Whatever." He removed his arm and stood.

Xander rose beside him.

Jim pulled his car keys from his coat pocket. "Wanna grab breakfast?"

"I'm exhausted. I need to shower and sleep. Maybe some other time."

Jim grunted and moved down the steps.

"No, wait—let's do it now," Xander said, bounding down the steps after his father.

AUTHOR'S NOTE

Xander, Terrance, Sunny, Jess, Charley and Buwan are the central characters in my novel *Beautiful and Terrible Things*, being published by Black Rose Writing in 2024. I invite you to spend more time with them in the full novel. Subscribe to my blog at AuthorSMStevens.com to receive notifications about the release schedule for *Beautiful and Terrible Things*. Thanks for reading, reviewing and sharing.

ACKNOWLEDGMENTS

Thank you to my beta readers Joseph Carrabis, Joe Della Rosa, Rox Burkey, Tina O'Hailey, Kristen Hamilton O'Neill, Alysan Sherota, Jen Stocks and Nancy White.

ALSO BY S.M. STEVENS

Horseshoes and Hand Grenades

Middle Grade:
Shannon's Odyssey

Young Adult:
Bit Players, Has-Been Actors and Other Posers
Bit Players, Bullies and Righteous Rebels
Bit Players, Bird Girls and Fake Break-Ups